REAL COWBOYS

KATE HOEFLER

Illustrated by

JONATHAN BEAN

HOUGHTON MIFFLIN HARCOURT
BOSTON   NEW YORK

For Arden and Jude—the faces I see
in the mountains I pass —K. H.

For Doug, Andrea, and their cowgirl
and cowboys —J.B.

Text copyright © 2016 by Kate Hoefler
Illustrations copyright © 2016 by Jonathon Bean

www.hmhco.com

The text of this book is set in Proxima Nova.
The illustrations are hand-stenciled shapes and textures layered
with the computer and printed in four Pantone colors.

Library of Congress Cataloging-in-Publication Data
Hoefler, Kate.
  Real cowboys / written by Kate Hoefler and illustrated by Jonathan Bean.
    pages cm
  Summary: Real cowboys are gentle, patient, and creative as they move
hundreds of cattle, make camp, and dream under the stars.
  ISBN 978-0-544-14892-5
  [1. Cowboys—Fiction.] I. Bean, Jonathan, 1979– illustrator. II. Title.
  PZ7.1.H62Re 2015
  [E]—dc23
                              2014048555

Manufactured in Malaysia
TWP 10 9 8 7 6 5 4 3 2 1
4500597793

Real cowboys are quiet in the morning, careful not to wake the people who live in little houses in the hollow, and up the mountains, and at the edge of fields in the distance.

Their work is to think of others: of the calf stranded on the ridge, and their dog coaxing it down—of how hundreds of moving cattle will feel about the sound of distant thunder.

Real cowboys are gentle. They know all the
songs that keep cattle calm, moving out of
storms, along dirt roads and narrow canyons.

At night, they sing lullabies over the calls
of coyotes—songs that keep cows
on a prairie deep in sleep.

They head to places called Stillwater or Red Town, but wherever they are, real cowboys are good listeners. They're always listening to their trail boss and to the other cowhands.

Sometimes they listen for trucks, and wolves, and rushing water. And sometimes they just listen to the big wide world and its grass song.

Real cowboys are safe. They pull their hats low because the sun can burn, and wear chaps so the cacti and brush don't cut them.

They're on cattle drives for hours,
or days, or weeks, but they don't mind.
Real cowboys are patient.

Even on a fast horse, they have to move with the slow rhythm of a herd, and it can take a long time to get places.

Real cowboys ask for help.
They use hand and hat signals
to let others know they need them,
and they ask their dogs for help too.
Real cowboys are good to their dogs.
They have a special way of talking to them.
Cowboys say "Go by" and "Look back,"
and their dogs listen, driving in a lost heifer.

Real cowboys want peace.
They don't want stampedes, where all the cattle
spook, and thunder over the earth,
and scatter in dust storms.

But sometimes it happens.

Some of those cattle and dogs are never found, and cowboys think of them from time to time when everything else on the prairie is quiet.

Real cowboys cry.

Real cowboys take turns. They make camp when the sun is as low as sagebrush, and eat in twos and threes at the chuck wagon. Later, they take turns watching over the cattle while others stretch out under mesquite moons.

Real cowboys are good to the earth.
They pick up their campsites, and keep
cattle moving to save water and grasslands.

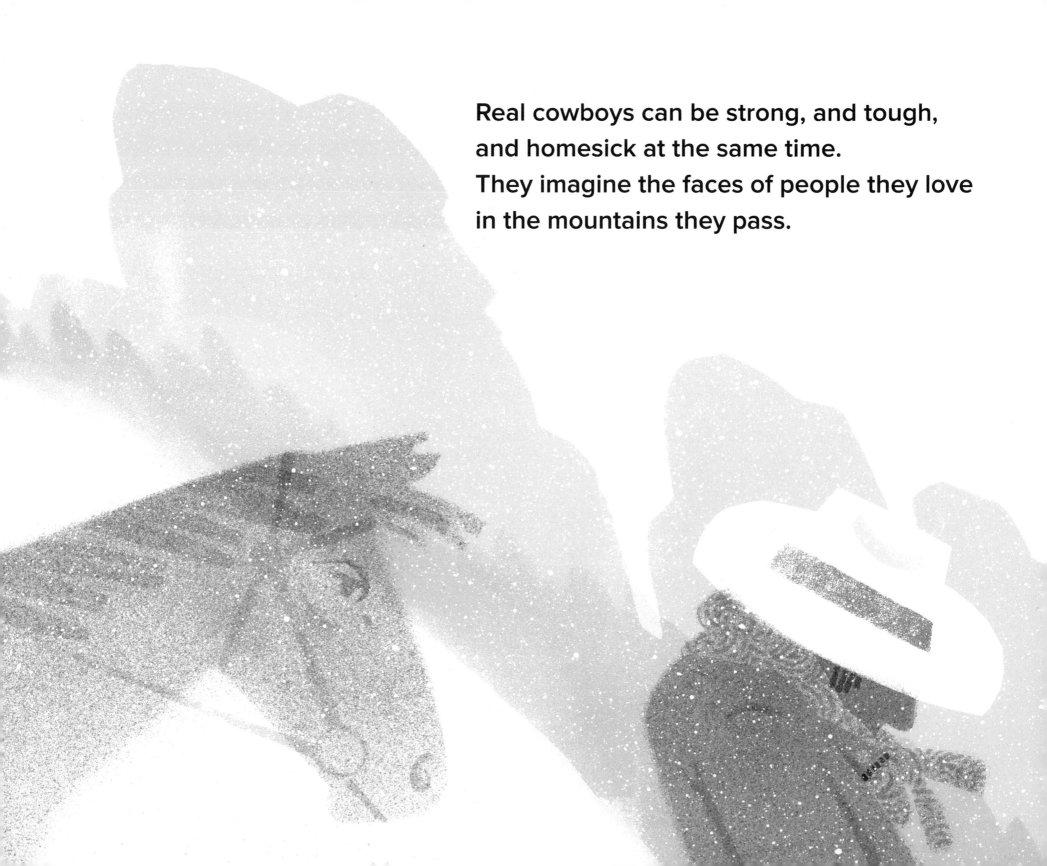

Real cowboys can be strong, and tough,
and homesick at the same time.
They imagine the faces of people they love
in the mountains they pass.

Real cowboys are as many different colors as the earth.

Real cowboys are girls, too.

Real cowboys are artists. They create.
They dream. They make up stories for their
friends, and horses, and dogs—stories about
the world that are bigger than moving cattle
to Stillwater or Red Town.

They sit under skies so big, the stars
take shape on the ground, and they wonder
what's past the horizon.

And one day, when their work is done, real cowboys find out.